MINI CLASSICS

THE PRINCESS
AND THE PEA

And The Red Shoes

RETOLD BY STEPHANIE LASLETT
ILLUSTRATED BY ALISON WINFIELD

||| •PARRAGON• |||

TITLES IN SERIES I AND II OF THE MINI CLASSICS INCLUDE:

SERIES I

SERIES II

Beauty and the Beast
Brer Rabbit and Brer Fox
A Christmas Carol
The Hare and the Tortoise
How the Leopard Got His Spots
Jack and the Beanstalk
The Magic Carpet
The Night Before Christmas
Pinocchio
Rapunzel
Red Riding Hood
The Secret Garden
The Selfish Giant
Sinbad the Sailor
The Snow Queen
The Steadfast Tin Soldier
Thumbelina
The Walrus and the Carpenter
The Wind in the Willows I
The Wind in the Willows II

A PARRAGON BOOK

Published by
Parragon Books,
Unit 13–17, Avonbridge Trading Estate,
Atlantic Road, Avonmouth, Bristol BS11 9QD

Produced by
The Templar Company plc,
Pippbrook Mill, London Road, Dorking, Surrey RH4 1JE

Designed by Mark Kingsley-Monks

Printed and bound in Great Britain

ISBN 1-85813-799-3

There was once a Prince, and the time came when he decided he wanted a wife. But his wife would have to be special. She had to be a real Princess. He travelled right around the world and met plenty of Princesses, but whether or not they were *real* Princesses he had great difficulty in discovering.

Each Princess was most attentive to the Prince, for he was handsome and kind and, as they all agreed, good Princes were hard to come by. After a while each Princess was invited to visit the palace and meet the King and Queen. But no matter how hard the eager Princesses tried, despite all their best efforts there was always

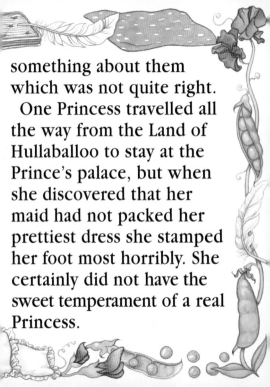

something about them which was not quite right.

One Princess travelled all the way from the Land of Hullaballoo to stay at the Prince's palace, but when she discovered that her maid had not packed her prettiest dress she stamped her foot most horribly. She certainly did not have the sweet temperament of a real Princess.

Another Princess came all the way from the Land of Blunderbuss, but as she took the Prince's arm for the Royal Waltz it was clear for all to see that she was not blessed with the grace of a real Princess.

Yet another Princess arrived from the Land of Scoffaroon but as she took her seat at the Royal Banquet it was sadly plain as day that she did not possess the manners of a real Princess.

11

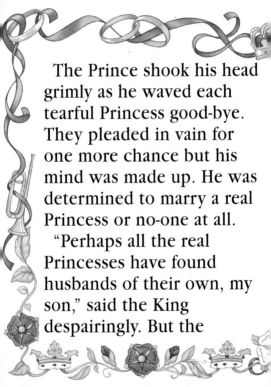

The Prince shook his head grimly as he waved each tearful Princess good-bye. They pleaded in vain for one more chance but his mind was made up. He was determined to marry a real Princess or no-one at all.

"Perhaps all the real Princesses have found husbands of their own, my son," said the King despairingly. But the

Prince did not reply. He knew that somewhere out there in the world was a real Princess waiting just for him.

So the weeks and months passed and to the King and Queen's dismay they were no nearer finding a bride for their son.

"Something has to be done. I must think of a plan," the Queen decided at last.

Up and down the battlements she paced with her chin in her hand and by the end of the day she had got it! *Now* she would be able to discover once and for all whether each Princess was a real Princess or not. Without telling a single soul, she climbed the twisting stairs to the guest bedroom and pulled all the bedclothes off the bed. Then she put her hand in her pocket and pulled out a small hard pea. Carefully she laid it on the mattress. Then she took twenty mattresses and piled them on top of the pea. Then she fetched twenty feather quilts and piled those on top of the mattresses until the bed was so high that you would need a ladder to climb into it!

That evening a new Princess arrived from the Land of Snozz and the Queen politely showed her to her room.

The next morning when the Princess came down for her breakfast of boiled eggs, she was greeted by the Queen.

"Good morning, my dear, and did you have a good night's sleep?" she asked.

"Wonderful!" replied the Princess. "What a lovely comfortable bed!" The Queen's shoulders drooped. This was not a real Princess.

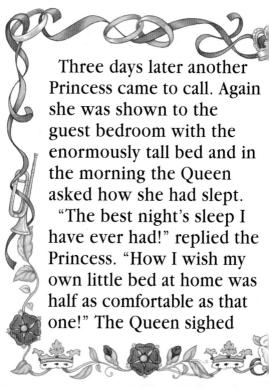

Three days later another Princess came to call. Again she was shown to the guest bedroom with the enormously tall bed and in the morning the Queen asked how she had slept.

"The best night's sleep I have ever had!" replied the Princess. "How I wish my own little bed at home was half as comfortable as that one!" The Queen sighed

heavily and wished her good day.

So it went on and to the Queen's great dismay, each Princess who came to call slept soundly in the bed with the twenty mattresses and the twenty feather quilts. More than ever before the Prince longed for a wife of his own but he began to despair of finding a real Princess.

One evening there was a
terrible storm. Thunder
shook the ground, forked
lightning split the sky and
rain poured down in
torrents. It was indeed a
fearful night. In the middle
of the storm, when the
thunder was at its loudest,
the lightning was at its
fiercest and the rain was at
its heaviest, a small knock
was heard at the town gate.

The old King was standing
on the battlements watching
the rain clouds roll across
the sky and he himself
went to open the door.

Outside was a young Princess, and she was drenched to the skin. The water streamed out of her hair and clothes, it ran in at the top of her shoes and out at the heel, but she said that she was a real Princess.

"Well we shall soon see if that is true," thought the Queen, but she said nothing and showed the Princess to her room.

Up the ladder climbed the Princess and gratefully she slipped between the soft white sheets. She lay her head upon the pillow and closed her eyes. But what was this? Something was not quite right.

In the morning the Prince and his mother and father waited anxiously over the boiled eggs in the breakfast-room.

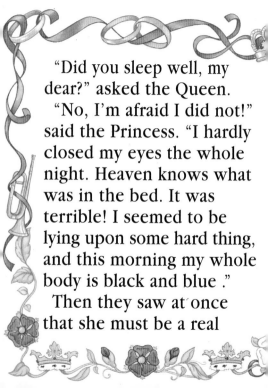

"Did you sleep well, my dear?" asked the Queen.

"No, I'm afraid I did not!" said the Princess. "I hardly closed my eyes the whole night. Heaven knows what was in the bed. It was terrible! I seemed to be lying upon some hard thing, and this morning my whole body is black and blue ."

Then they saw at once that she must be a real

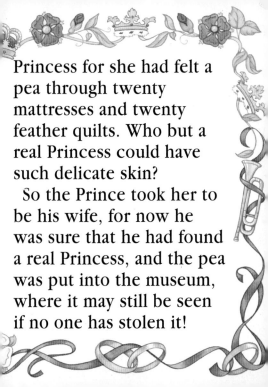

Princess for she had felt a pea through twenty mattresses and twenty feather quilts. Who but a real Princess could have such delicate skin?

So the Prince took her to be his wife, for now he was sure that he had found a real Princess, and the pea was put into the museum, where it may still be seen if no one has stolen it!

There was once a little girl who was very poor. In the winter she had just one pair of heavy wooden shoes which rubbed at the skin on her ankles and made them terribly sore, but in the summer she always went barefoot.

An old mother shoemaker lived in the middle of the village and she decided to make a pair of shoes for the little girl, whose name was Karen. She stitched together some strips of old brown cloth and soon the shoes were finished. They were very rough and ready, but they had been made by a good heart and with the best will in the world.

Karen was delighted by her new shoes and decided to save them for a special occasion. But the first chance that came for her to wear them was a very sad day. Her poor mother caught a fever and died. On the day of the funeral Karen had no black shoes to wear and so she wore her brown shoes as she walked behind the coffin.

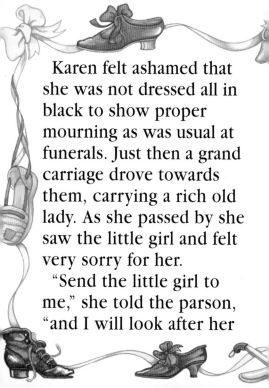

Karen felt ashamed that she was not dressed all in black to show proper mourning as was usual at funerals. Just then a grand carriage drove towards them, carrying a rich old lady. As she passed by she saw the little girl and felt very sorry for her.

"Send the little girl to me," she told the parson, "and I will look after her and be kind to her." Karen thought it was all because the old lady had admired her brown shoes, but the lady said they were horrid and soon had them burnt. She bought Karen a pair of boots and from then on the little girl was well cared for. People said she was pretty, but her mirror said, "You are more than pretty — you are lovely."

One day Karen heard that
the Queen and her daughter,
the little Princess, were
staying in their country
palace nearby.

Karen waited a whole day
outside the railings, hoping
to catch a glimpse of the
Royal family, and then, to
her great delight, she
caught a glimpse of the
little Princess standing at
the window.

She was dressed all in white with a beautiful pair of soft red leather shoes upon her feet. Karen looked at her own black boots. How she wished they were the same as the Princess's pretty slippers!

The years passed quickly by and soon the time arrived when Karen was old enough to be confirmed in the church.

She was given new clothes and promised a pair of new shoes. As the shoemaker measured her little foot, Karen looked around at the sparkling glass cases of beautiful shoes and shiny leather boots.

"How lovely they are!" said Karen, but the old lady could not see very well, so it gave her no pleasure to look at them.

Suddenly Karen gasped.
There was a pair of shoes
nearly as pretty as those
worn by the Princess. Oh,
how lovely they were!

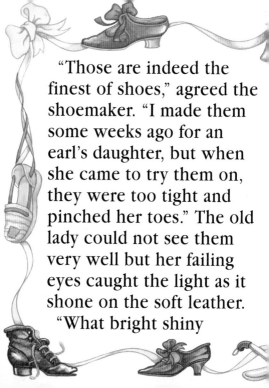

"Those are indeed the finest of shoes," agreed the shoemaker. "I made them some weeks ago for an earl's daughter, but when she came to try them on, they were too tight and pinched her toes." The old lady could not see them very well but her failing eyes caught the light as it shone on the soft leather. "What bright shiny

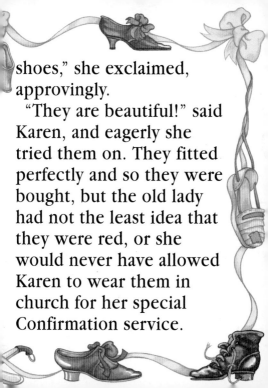

shoes," she exclaimed, approvingly.

"They are beautiful!" said Karen, and eagerly she tried them on. They fitted perfectly and so they were bought, but the old lady had not the least idea that they were red, or she would never have allowed Karen to wear them in church for her special Confirmation service.

On Sunday Karen walked proudly into church in her new shoes. Everybody stared at her feet.

Down either side of the church hung old portraits of dead and gone parsons and their wives, with stiff collars and long black clothes. As she walked down the aisle Karen felt as if their eyes were watching her every footstep. She could think of nothing else when the priest laid his hand upon her head and spoke to her of holy baptism and that from henceforth she was to be a responsible Christian person. The solemn notes of the organ filled the air, the children in the choir sang with sweet voices, but Karen could only think of her shoes.

By that afternoon all the villagers had told the old lady just how unsuitable the red shoes had been.

"That is very naughty and most improper!" she told Karen. "In future, you will wear black shoes to church, even if they are old." Next Sunday Karen was to receive Holy Communion for the first time. She looked at the red shoes and then at the black ones — then she looked again at the red, and at last she put them on.

It was a beautiful sunny day and Karen and the old lady took the dusty path through the cornfield. By the church door stood an old soldier leaning on a crutch. He had a strange long beard, almost pure red in colour. He bent down and asked the old lady if he might dust her shoes. Then Karen put out her little foot, too.

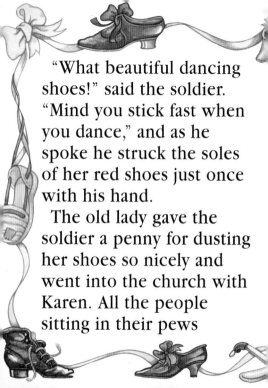

"What beautiful dancing shoes!" said the soldier. "Mind you stick fast when you dance," and as he spoke he struck the soles of her red shoes just once with his hand.

The old lady gave the soldier a penny for dusting her shoes so nicely and went into the church with Karen. All the people sitting in their pews looked at Karen's red shoes, and all the portraits looked hard at them too.

When Karen knelt at the altar-rails and the chalice was put to her lips, she could think only of the red shoes; she seemed to see them floating in front of her eyes. She forgot to join in the hymn of praise and she forgot to say the Lord's Prayer.

After the service, everybody left the church and the old lady got into her carriage. As Karen followed her down the path, she passed the old soldier. "Look at the pretty dancing shoes!" he said. Suddenly something happened to Karen's feet. She took a few dancing steps and suddenly found her feet would not stop.

It was just as if the shoes had a power over them. She danced right round the church two times! The coachman had to run after her and lift her into the carriage, but Karen's feet continued to dance, and she kicked the poor old lady most horribly. At last the coachman pulled the shoes off, and her poor feet finally got some rest.

When they got home the shoes were put away in a cupboard and she was forbidden to wear them ever again, but Karen could not help going to peek at them from time to time.

The weeks passed, and after a time the old lady became very ill. The doctor said she would not live much longer and would need to be carefully nursed. Karen lived with the old lady and so it was decided that she would take care of her.

The very next day there was to be a grand ball in the town. Karen looked at the old lady. "I would dearly love to go to the ball," she thought, "and the old lady does not have long to live so it should not matter to her whether I stay or go." She went to the cupboard and looked longingly at the red shoes. "There is no harm in looking," she said, but soon she wanted to do more than look. "I will just try them on," she said.

But as soon as she had tied the bows, she found herself skipping to the ball — and there she began to dance! The shoes would not let her do as she liked.

When she wanted to go to the right, they danced to the left. When she wanted to dance up the room, the shoes danced down the room, then down the stairs,

through the streets, and out
of the town gate. Away she
danced, and away she *had*
to dance, deep into the dark
forest. High in the sky
something shone above the
trees. Karen thought it was
the moon but to her great
surprise she saw it was the
old soldier with the red
beard. Slowly he nodded
and said, "Look at the
pretty dancing shoes!"

The sight of this strange vision frightened Karen terribly and she tried to pull off the red shoes. She tore off her stockings but the shoes had grown fast to her feet and off she danced, and off she *had* to dance over fields and meadows, in sunshine and in rain, by day and by night, and at night it was especially fearful.

She danced into the open churchyard, but the dead did not join her dance for they had something more pressing to do. She wanted to sit down on a pauper's grave where the bitter wormwood grew, but there was no rest for her there. As she danced towards the open church door she saw an angel in long white robes and golden wings and his face was stern. In his hand he held a broad shining sword.

"Dance you shall!" said the angel. "You shall dance in your red shoes till you are pale and cold. You shall dance from door to door, and wherever you find vain proud children you must knock at their door so that they can see you and fear you. Yes, you shall dance!"

"Mercy!" shrieked Karen, but she did not hear the angel's reply, for the shoes bore her through the gate, into the fields, over roadways and along paths. Ever and ever onwards she was forced to dance.

One morning she danced past a door she knew well for it was her old home. She heard the sound of a hymn from within and a coffin covered with flowers was carried down the path. Then she knew that the old lady was dead and it seemed to her that she was forsaken by all the world and cursed by the holy angels of God.

On and ever on she danced, and dance she must, even through the long dark nights. The shoes bore her away over briars and stubble till her feet were torn and bleeding. She danced away over the heath till she came to a lonely little house. She knew the executioner lived there and she tapped with her fingers on the window pane and said, "Come out! Come out! I can't come in for I am dancing!"

The executioner said, "Do you know who I am? I chop off the bad people's heads and I see that my axe has begun to quiver."

"Please don't chop off my head," cried Karen, "but, pray chop my feet off for the red shoes will give me no peace at all!"

Then she confessed all her sins and admitted her foolish pride and vanity. The executioner chopped off her feet, but the red shoes kept on dancing till they were far out of sight.

"Thank you," said Karen.
"At last I am free!" Then
the executioner made her a
pair of little wooden legs
and crutches.

"I have suffered enough
for those red shoes," she
said. "Now I will go to
church so that everyone
can see that my shoes have
gone." But as she arrived at
the door, the red shoes
danced up in front of her!

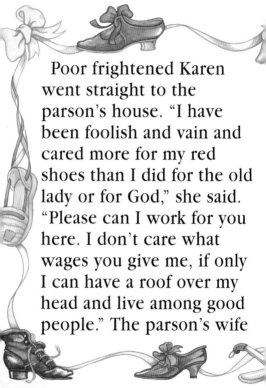

Poor frightened Karen went straight to the parson's house. "I have been foolish and vain and cared more for my red shoes than I did for the old lady or for God," she said. "Please can I work for you here. I don't care what wages you give me, if only I can have a roof over my head and live among good people." The parson's wife felt sorry for her, and took her into her house and Karen proved to be a kind and hardworking little girl. The Parson's little ones were very fond of her but when they chattered about lovely dresses and soft leather shoes, and how they longed to be as beautiful as a queen, she would shake her head and sigh.

Next Sunday the children went to church and they asked Karen to go with them. Sadly she looked at her crutches and shook her head, and whilst they knelt to hear the word of God, she sat in her little room all alone.

Silently Karen bowed her head and clasping her hands together she began to pray.

As Karen prayed, she heard the notes of the church organ borne on the wind and she raised her tear-stained face. "Oh, God, help me!" she cried.

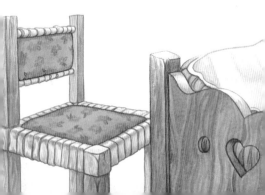

Then the sun shone brightly around her, and the angel in the white robes stood before her. He no longer held the sharp sword in his hand but a beautiful green branch covered with roses.

The angel reached out and gently touched the ceiling with his hand. Slowly the roof rose higher and higher and wherever the angel touched his hand, a bright golden star appeared and shone down upon Karen. Then he touched the walls and they spread far apart. Sweet music could be heard and it grew louder and louder.

Soon Karen was astonished to see the church organ. She saw the paintings of the parsons and their wives and there was the congregation sitting in their seats and singing aloud. When the hymn came to an end they looked up and nodded to her and said, "We are glad you came to church after all, little Karen!"

"It was through God's mercy!" she said. The organ played, and the children's voices echoed sweetly through the choir.

The warm rays of sun streamed in through the window and lit up the bench where little Karen sat in wonder. Her heart was so full of the sunshine, the perfect peace, and sudden overwhelming joy that it broke. Then her soul flew with the warm sunbeams to heaven, and no-one there ever asked her about the red shoes.

HANS CHRISTIAN ANDERSEN

Hans Andersen was born in
Odense, Denmark on April 2nd, 1805.
His family was very poor and
throughout his life he suffered much
unhappiness. Even after he found
success as a writer, Hans Andersen
felt something of an outsider,
an attitude which can be seen
in many of his fairy stories.
The Princess and the Pea is thought
to be a very old Swedish folk tale,
retold by Hans Andersen and
published in his first collection
of stories in 1836.